Blue Whales

16.95

599.5248
MCDO

Blue
Whales

Mary Ann McDonald

THE CHILD'S WORLD®, INC.

HUNTINGTON BEACH PUBLIC LIBRARY
7111 Talbert Avenue
Huntington Beach, CA 92648

Copyright © 1998 by The Child's World®, Inc.
All rights reserved. No part of this book may be
reproduced or utilized in any form or by any means
without written permission from the publisher.
Printed in the United States of America.

Library of Congress Cataloging-in-Publication Data
McDonald, Mary Ann
Blue whales / by Mary Ann McDonald
p.   cm.
Includes index.
Summary: Describes the physical characteristics, behavior,
and habitat of the largest animal on Earth, the blue whale.
ISBN 1-56766-472-5 (lib. reinforced : alk. paper)
1. Blue whale—Juvenile literature.
[1. Blue whale. 2. Whales.]   I. Title.
QL737.C424M315   1998
599.5'248—dc21   97-38098
CIP
AC

Photo Credits

ANIMALS ANIMALS © C.J. Gilbert: 15
© Daniel J. Cox/Natural Exposures: 13, 16, 23
© Joe McDonald: 20
© Marilyn Kazmers/Sharksong: 2
© Russ Kinne/Comstock, Inc.: cover, 6, 10, 24, 26
© Peter Howorth/Tom Campbell's Photographic: 9, 19, 29, 30

On the cover...

Front cover: This blue whale is swimming alone.
Page 2: This blue whale is diving down deep.

Table of Contents

The ocean is full of life. Dolphins and killer whales swim near the surface. Sharks, eels, and fish swim deeper down. In the distance, a huge animal appears. As it swims closer, it moves its giant head and pumps its tail. What could this animal be? It's a blue whale!

⇐ This huge blue whale is surfacing for air.

What Are Blue Whales?

Blue whales belong to the same animal group as dolphins. These animals are called **mammals**. Mammals have warm blood and breathe air. They also feed their babies milk from their bodies. Dogs, monkeys, and people are mammals, too.

Most mammals have hair on their bodies, but blue whales do not. Over thousands of years, their bodies have slowly changed. Instead of being covered with fur, blue whales have bare, shiny skin. This smooth skin lets them swim easily through the water.

This blue whale's skin is very smooth. ⇒

What Do Blue Whales Look Like?

Blue whales are the largest animals on Earth. They can grow to be 100 feet long and weigh almost 320,000 pounds. In fact, baby blue whales, called **calves**, are already 20 feet long when they are born! They grow very fast and can gain up to 195 pounds every day. By the time they are eight months old, blue whale calves are almost 50 feet long.

⟸ It is easy to see how big blue whales really are.

Blue whales get their name from their bluish gray color. They have huge, rounded bodies and powerful tails. Instead of arms, blue whales have two **flippers** that look like paddles. The flippers help the whale change direction underwater. Blue whales also have a tiny fin on their backs. This fin is called a **dorsal fin**. It keeps the whale from tipping over while it is swimming.

Blue whales like this one have tiny dorsal fins. ⇒

What Do Blue Whales Eat?

Since blue whales are so large, they must eat lots of food every day. The blue whale's favorite food is **krill**. Krill are tiny pink animals that live in the ocean. Many people think they look like little shrimp. There are countless millions of krill in the world's oceans. Sometimes there are so many krill in one place, the ocean looks pink!

This tiny krill is in danger of being eaten by a blue whale. ⇒

How Do Blue Whales Eat?

Blue whales do not have teeth. Instead, they have hundreds of small rows hanging down from the tops of their mouths. These rows are called **baleen**. Baleen is made of the same material as your fingernails. Baleen is smooth on the outside and has tiny hairs on the inside. Water passes easily through baleen. But other things, such as krill or water plants, get caught in the tiny hairs.

⇐ This *humpback whale* has baleen just as blue whales do.

To catch krill, a blue whale simply opens its mouth underwater. In one big gulp, the whale's mouth fills up with lots of water—and lots of krill! The whale's huge throat stretches to hold all of the water. Then the whale quickly shuts its mouth. The water drains out through the baleen, but the krill get caught in the little hairs. Soon, all that's left in the whale's mouth are thousands of little krill.

This blue whale's throat is full of water and krill. ⇒

How Do Blue Whales Breathe?

Blue whales need to breathe air just as you do. But instead of breathing through their noses, blue whales use something called a **blowhole**. A blowhole is a hole in the top of the whale's head. When a whale dives underwater, it holds its breath and closes its blowhole. When the whale comes up to breathe, it opens the blowhole to let air in.

⇐ This blue whale's blowhole is open to breathe in air.

Do Blue Whales Sleep?

When blue whales sleep, it is called **logging**. When a blue whale is logging, it rests just under the surface of the water. It slowly floats to the surface when it needs to breathe. After taking several breaths, it slowly sinks back under the water. Blue whales usually sleep during the middle of the day.

This blue whale is logging in the warm waters of Mexico. ⇒

Do Blue Whales Talk?

Blue whales are the loudest animals in the world. In fact, some scientists say that a blue whale can make sounds as loud as a jet plane! Blue whales use these sounds to talk to each other. The whales use these loud, low sounds to talk to each other—even if they are very far apart.

⇐ These blue whales are sending loud sounds through the water.

Where Do Blue Whales Live?

Blue whales spend much of their time in colder waters. There they can find plenty of krill to eat. But when winter comes, the water in these areas becomes too cold. The blue whales must move south. In warmer waters, they can find more food to eat. They can also safely have their babies.

⇐ These blue whales are swimming to warmer waters.

Do Blue Whales Have Any Enemies?

Blue whales do not have many enemies. They are just too big! Sometimes *killer whales* hunt and eat blue whales if there is nothing else to eat. But the blue whales' biggest enemy is people. Because of hunting and damage to the areas in which they live, blue whales have been in danger for many years.

Killer whales like this one sometimes eat blue whales. ⇒

Today, many people are trying to help the blue whales. But there is still much to be done. We must make sure we keep our oceans clean. We must also protect the krill and other animals the whales need to eat. If we work to protect the blue whales, these beautiful giants will be around for a very long time.

Glossary

baleen (buh–LEEN)
Baleen is a kind of screen that blue whales have in their mouths. Baleen keeps the food in and lets water out.

blowhole (BLOH–hole)
Blue whales breathe through a blowhole. The blowhole keeps water out when the whale is underwater.

calves (KAVZ)
Baby blue whales are called calves. Blue whale calves are very large.

dorsal fin (DOR–sull FIN)
Many whales and fish have a dorsal fin on their backs. It keeps them from tipping over while they are swimming.

flippers (FLIH–perz)
Flippers are a whale's "arms." They work like paddles to help the whale change directions underwater.

krill (KRILL)
Krill are tiny water animals. Blue whales love to eat krill.

logging (LOG–ging)
When blue whales sleep, it is called logging. Blue whales usually log in the middle of the day.

mammals (MA–mullz)
Mammals are animals that feed their babies milk from their bodies. Blue whales, dogs, monkeys, and people are mammals.

Index